# Ghosts and Poltergeists

by Gisela Meier

**Published By
Capstone Press, Inc.
Mankato, Minnesota USA**

**Distributed By**

 CHILDRENS PRESS ®

CHICAGO

# CIP
## LIBRARY OF CONGRESS CATALOGING IN PUBLICATION DATA

Meier, Gisela.
Ghosts and poltergeists / by Gisela Meier.
p. cm. – (The Unexplained)
Summary: Examines evidence supporting the existence of ghosts and poltergeists.

ISBN 1-56065-040-0:
1. Ghosts – Juvenile literature. 2. Poltergeists – Juvenile literature. [1. Ghosts. 2. Poltergeists.] I. Title. II. Series.
BF1461.M45     1989
133.1 – dc20                                                89-27799
                                                                 CIP
                                                                 AC

## PHOTO CREDITS

Capstone Press: 4, 8, 15, 19, 23, 36, 38, 41
The Children's Theatre: 32
The Guthrie Theater: 10, 34, 44

## CAPSTONE PRESS
Box 669, Mankato, MN 56001

# Contents

# Introduction

The little girl was alone in the big bed in a strange house in London. She was crying.

Her name was Kitty. For as long as she could remember, she had lived with her grandparents here in England. Two days ago, her mother had come to get her. They would be living together in Heidelberg, Germany. Her mother had a job there.

They were spending a few days in the home of a friend. He was a photographer and a widower with a young son. Tonight, Kitty's mother had gone to the theatre. Every now and then the little boy's nanny looked into the bedroom to check on Kitty.

For a long time, Kitty sobbed. She was lonely and frightened. She missed her grandparents. She did not want to go to Germany with her mother, whom she hardly knew.

Someone came into the room. It was not the nanny. It was a beautiful young woman with long, red hair. She wore a lovely blue satin dressing gown.

She sat down on the bed and stroked Kitty's hair.

"Your Mommy has gone out, but she'll be back soon," the woman said. "I will stay with you until she gets back."

Kitty wiped her eyes and sniffed. She listened while the woman spoke softly to her. The woman talked about how much Kitty's mother loved her. She said it really was better for her to live with her mother.

The next time the nanny peeked into the bedroom, Kitty was sleeping. A smile was on her face.

In the morning, Kitty told her mother all about the woman. Puzzled, her mother asked the nanny about the woman.

The nanny gasped and turned pale. The photographer's wife, she said, had been a beautiful woman with long red hair. She had been very unhappy, perhaps mentally ill. She was wearing a blue satin dressing gown when she died. She had thrown herself from the balcony of the bedroom where Kitty had slept.

Kitty's mother said this actually happened in 1952. She told the story to ghosthunter Hans Holzer. He wrote about it in one of his books about ghosts.

People have been telling each other ghost tales for thousands of years. The first ghost stories were probably told around the campfires of prehistoric humans. At every time in history and in every part of the world, people have believed in ghosts.

Today, we are still haunted by ghosts. We see them in our books, our movies, and our cartoons. Some of us see them in our homes.

Are they real? There are people who are trying to find out. They are called **psychical** (sy-kik-ul) or **parapsychologists** (pair-a-sy-kil-oh-jists). Many of them are very serious in their search for ghosts.

So far, they haven't come up with any real answers. But they are still looking.

# A Variety of Ghosts

When you say "ghost," most people think of something wrapped in sheets. It wanders through a spooky house at midnight and moans a lot. There are many stories about ghosts that look like this. There are many other kinds of ghosts, too.

Ancient stories tell of ghosts that looked like horned, fire-breathing giants or large, fierce animals. The ghosts in some tales sound like they have just crawled out of a grave. They look like rotting corpses or skeletons wrapped in burial sheets.

Other ghosts carry signs of their death. The ghost of a drowning victim who haunted a New Orleans bridge was draped in seaweed. The ghost of Ann Boleyn, who was beheaded by order of King Henry VIII, is said to wander through the Tower of London with her head tucked under her arm.

People are not the only ones who come back to haunt the living. Many stories tell of ghostly dogs, cats, horses, and other animals. There are also legends about phantom ships and ghostly trains.

Most of these stories are hundreds of years old. The

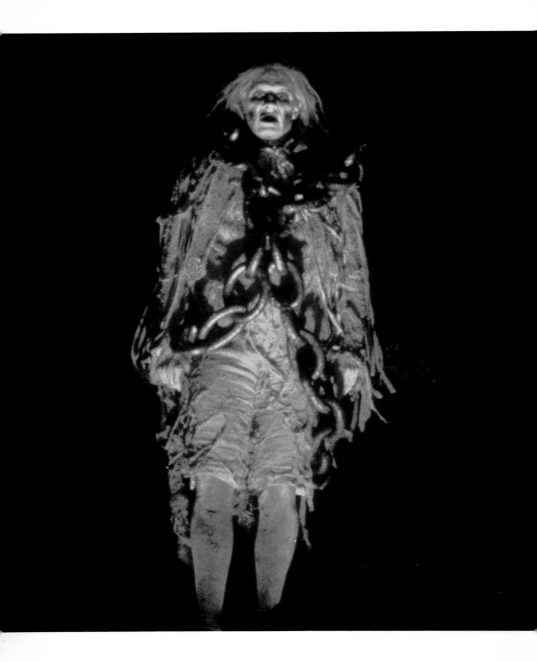

ghosts that appear in most modern stories are not as strange. Usually, they look like normal humans. They may talk to people and even touch them. Sometimes people don't know they are dealing with a ghost until it disappears.

Han holzer tells one such story in his book, ***Ghosts of the Golden West***:

"It happened in 1928 in Palo Alto, California...on Emerson Street. Ralph Madison was minding his own business, walking when he noticed a man named Knight, whom he knew slightly. The two men stopped to talk and Madison shook hands with the other man.

"It struck him as peculiar, however, that the man's voice seemed unusually wispy. Moreover, Knight's hands were clammy and cold!

"They exchanged some words and then they parted. Madison started out again and then quickly glanced around at his friend. The man he had just shaken hands with had disappeared into thin air. At this moment, he suddenly remembered that Mr. Knight had been dead and buried for five years."

As this story shows, ghosts do not appear only in gloomy castles or creepy old houses. They do not show up only on dark and stormy nights. Ghosts have been seen in open fields, on ships, in apartments, in a Beverly Hills mansion, in a bakery, and in a bathroom.

Several ghosts are said to **haunt** the Drury Lane Theatre in London. One is a handsome young man in an elegant 18th-century outfit. He has been seen many times working alone on a balcony during rehearsals. Another ghost supposedly helps young performers by gently guiding them about the stage with unseen hands.

Ghosts have even been seen on jumbo jets. In 1973 and 1974 several Eastern Airlines jets were haunted by two phantoms. John G. Fuller wrote a book about the case, called ***The Ghost of Flight 401.***

The ghosts were Captain Bob Loft and flight engineer Don Repo. They were killed when Eastern Airlines Flight 401 crashed in the Miami Everglades on December 29, 1972.

In the months after the crash, Fuller reports, Loft and Repo were seen many times by pilots, engineers, flight attendants, repairmen, and passengers on Eastern Airlines planes.

One time, a stewardess was counting passengers on a jet that was preparing for take-off. Sitting in the first class section was a man who was not on her passenger list. He was wearing an Eastern captain's uniform. As a few other passengers watched, she tried to talk to the man. He would not answer. Puzzled, she went to the cockpit and asked the flight captain to come back to the first class section.

According to Fuller, this is what happened next:

"With both the stewardess and the flight supervisor beside him, the flight captain leaned down to address the other captain. Then he froze. 'My God, it's Bob Loft,' he said. There was silence in the cabin. Then something happened that no one could explain. The captain in the first-class seat simply was not there. He was there one moment and not there the next."

There were also stories that flight engineer Repo had appeared. His spirit seemed to be very concerned with the safety of the jumbo jets that he had loved to fly. Several times he warned crew members about mechanical problems on the planes. The problems turned out to be real.

Eastern Airlines officials insisted that the stories were only rumors. They said that they had no real reports about the ghosts.

# Crisis Apparitions

Many ghost stories tell of a person who appears to a distant friend or relative. Later, it turns out that the person died at the same time. This is sometimes called a "crisis **apparition**" (ap-pair-in´-shun).

One of the most interesting crisis apparitions happened at the end of World War I. It involved Lieutenant David McConnell, an 18-year-old British pilot.

On December 7, 1918, McConnell was flying a small plane from his home base in Scampton, England to a field at Tadcaster, England about 60 miles away. He tried to land in a heavy fog, but crashed. McConnell was killed. The impact broke his watch. It recorded the time of his death at 3:25 p.m.

Back in Scampton, McConnell's roommate, Lieutenant Larkin, was sitting in their room alone. He was reading and smoking. Sometime between 3:15 and 3:30 p.m., Larkin heard footsteps in the hall. The door behind him opened.

"Hello, boy!" a familiar voice said.

Looking up, Larkin saw McConnell standing in the doorway, about eight feet away.

"Hello," Larkin replied. "Back already?"

"Yes," the other said. "Got there all right. Had a good trip. Well, cheerio!"

McConnell left, closing the door behind him.

A short time later, another officer, Lieutenant Garner Smith, came into the room. Smith said he hoped McConnell would be back soon so that the three of them could go someplace that night. Larkin said that he had already seen McConnell within the past half hour.

Later that evening Larkin learned of McConnell's death. He realized he had seen his friend at the time he died. Larkin told several people, including McConnell's parents, about what he had seen.

Was Larkin dreaming? He insisted he was awake when he saw McConnell. He was awake when Smith came into the room a short time later.

Was Larkin playing a trick on Smith? Larkin did not know about McConnell's death until much later. It is very unlikely that the two young pilots would plan a joke involving something as serious as the death of their friend. Still, McConnell could not have been in his room when Larkin saw him.

Then who—or what—was standing in the doorway?

Some psychical researchers believe that a crisis appari-

tion is actually a case of **mental telepathy** (tel-eh´-path-ee). Mental telepathy is the ability to communicate without using sight, sound or actions. Some people seem to be able to do this. They know what another person is thinking or doing, even if that person is far away. The person who sees the ghost "senses" the other person's death through mental telepathy. He then creates a **hallucination** (hal-oo´-sin-ay´shun) of the ghost. This means he thinks he sees the other person, but it is really just his mind playing tricks on him.

Other parapsychologists believe that everyone has a spirit. This spirit leaves the body when the person dies. The spirit is what people see when a ghost appears to them.

Some people believe the spirit can leave a person's body even during life. There are many stories involving the "ghosts" of living people.

In one case, an English woman dreamed for many nights that she was walking through an old country house. Later, she and her husband visited a large estate in Scotland. She recognized it as the house in her dreams. She could describe various rooms before she walked into them.

The owner of the estate was shocked when he met the woman. He said she looked just like a ghost that had been seen walking through the house.

# Haunts

While some ghosts talk to people, others take no notice of the living. They act as if they were sleepwalking. This type of ghost is sometimes called a haunt. It appears again and again at the same place, going through the same motions each time.

A haunt usually wears clothing from the past. The body may look transparent. In a house, it may walk through furniture and walls.

A classic haunt case began in 1882 in a large Victorian house in Cheltenham, England. Many researchers say it is the most reliable report about a ghost. This is because the main witness, Rosina Despard, was a very intelligent young woman who later became a doctor.

The ghost Rosina saw was a tall lady. She was dressed in black, with a handkerchief in one hand. She seemed to be solid. She never spoke and made no sound except for footsteps. She would show up suddenly at any time of the day or night. Then, just as suddenly, she would disappear.

Many other people said they saw the ghost during the next seven years. There were even times when one person in the room saw the ghost and the others did not. Dogs in the house also reacted to the ghost and cats did not.

The Whaley House is a historical building in San Diego, California. It is home to a number of haunts. The house was built in the 1850s. It has been turned into a museum. Employees and visitors at the museum say they have seen ghosts. The ghosts are of a small, dark-skinned woman in a long full skirt, a man wearing an old-fashioned suit, and a small spotted dog, among others. One woman saw a room full of ghostly men walking around and talking to each other.

In December, 1972, Time magazine had a report about a haunt at the United States Military Academy at West Point, New York. Two cadets living in one of the barracks said that they had both seen the ghost of a soldier. He was wearing a uniform from the early nineteenth century.

A few days later, Cadet Captain Keith Bakken and another student at the academy spent the night in the same room. The ghost appeared to Bakken's friend and then vanished back into the wall. Bakken did not see the ghost, but the spot where the ghost had disappeared felt icy to the touch.

Some parapsychologists believe that haunts are not the souls of dead people. Somehow, a sort of memory or image of the person gets stuck in time, although the person goes on to other things. When people see a haunt, it is like watching someone on television. The image they see is not alive or aware.

Other researchers believe that in some way we do not yet understand, the past still exists. People who see a haunt are actually looking into the past.

# The Ghosts of Washington D.C.

The most famous haunted mansion in the United States is the White House. American Presidents have lived there since 1800. The ghosts of several famous Americans have been seen there.

One is Abigail Adams, wife of John Adams, America's second President. Some people have watched her walk through locked doors, others have seen her doing laundry in the East Room, just as she did when she was alive.

Dolley Madison is said to have returned to the White House nearly 100 years after the term of her husband James Madison. President Woodrow Wilson's wife had ordered the White House gardeners to move Dolley's rose garden. They were about to begin digging when the ghost of Dolley rushed up and scolded them. They dropped their shovels, and the rose garden stayed where it was.

The most famous ghost at the White House is President Abraham Lincoln, who was killed in 1865. For years after his death, people said they heard his footsteps around the mansion. Grace Coolidge, the wife of Calvin Coolidge, said she saw Lincoln staring out of an Oval Office window when she lived in the White House. This was 60 years after Lincoln's death.

There were many reports about Lincoln's ghost during the presidency of Franklin D. Roosevelt. Eleanor Roosevelt is said to have felt his presence behind her as she worked at her desk. A secretary who worked at the White House said she saw Lincoln sitting on the bed in his old bedroom. He was pulling on his boots.

When Queen Wilhelmina of the Netherlands came for a visit during Roosevelt's term, she stayed in Lincoln's bedroom. One night, there was a knock at the door. The queen opened it. There stood Lincoln, wearing his top hat.

When the queen told Roosevelt about it the next morning, he did not seem surprised. He said many others had seen Lincoln in or near that room.

Lincoln's ghost still may wander through the White House. President Ronald Reagan's daughter Maureen, slept in the Lincoln Bedroom when she came to visit. She said she and her husband saw a light, late at night. Sometimes it was orange, sometimes red. They believed it was Lincoln's spirit.

President Reagan and his wife Nancy never saw Lincoln's ghost. However, Nancy said that Rex, the family dog, often barked at the door to the Lincoln Bedroom and refused to go in.

# Poltergeists

The term **poltergeist** (pole'-ter-guyst) comes from two German words: polter meaning "noise," and geist, meaning "ghost." No one has seen a poltergeist.

It began when a few flowerpots fell off the shelves during the night. Beulah Wilson didn't think much of it. You can expect to hear odd noises at night with a frisky cat in the house. Besides, Mrs. Wilson was a widow and had a lot to do. She had taken a 9-year-old foster son into her home. Christmas was coming and she wanted to make it a special holiday for the boy.

She was busy in the kitchen on December 19. A banana and an orange fell from the top of a kitchen cabinet. Blaming the cat, she put the fruit back on the cabinet. She turned her back, and both pieces plopped to the floor again.

Then the Christmas tree in the living room fell over. Lamps fell off tables. Furniture turned upside down. Dishes were shattered. A heavy, old-fashioned sewing machine tipped over.

The police were called. They arrived about 45 minutes later to find the house was in a shambles. They had no idea what had caused that much damage. The police decided it could not have been Mrs. Wilson or the boy.

Some of the objects were much too heavy for a 65-year-old woman or a 9-year-old boy to move.

The police called Dr. J. Gaither Pratt, a psychical researcher from the University of Virginia. After visiting the house, Dr. Pratt told the police what had wrecked Mrs. Wilson's house.

He said it was a poltergeist.

Of all the kinds of ghosts, the poltergeist is said to be the strangest. Parapsychologists say a poltergeist usually starts by making tapping or scratching sounds in a house. This is followed by loud bangs and crashing noises. Doors may open and close by themselves. Lights flash on and off. Objects fall or are thrown across a room. Sometimes they move in slow motion, as if they are being carried. Objects may also fly in a zigzag path, moving around furniture and corners.

In some cases, stones or other objects seem to come from nowhere. People who pick up something that was tossed by a poltergeist often say it feels warm.

Poltergeist cases usually do not last very long. Most end within a few days or weeks.

Some poltergeists seem to like a particular activity. In 1958, the Herrmann family of Seaford, Long Island, had a poltergeist that zeroed in on all the bottles in the house. Caps on bottles seemed to unscrew themselves or pop off. Bottles of water, shampoo, perfume, bleach, and medicine were spilled or broken. This poltergeist also seemed to enjoy tossing small ceramic statues until they broke.

In 1963, the Yale family of Methuen, Massachusetts, had to deal with a water-squirting poltergeist. Water suddenly shot from the walls of the rooms. Water bubbles the size of marbles beaded up on the furniture. The main water supply to the house was turned off. All the pipes were drained. Still the water kept squirting. This lasted only one week.

The deeds of a poltergeist do not always occur in a house. In January, 1967, there was a case in a warehouse in Miami, Florida. The warehouse was owned by a company that sold souvenirs and knickknacks. Hundreds of glasses, ashtrays, toys, and other trinkets dropped from the shelves when no one was around. Entire boxes full of items slid off the shelves.

The warehouse was checked by police, a magician, and two parapsychologists. None of them found a natural cause for the mess.

In nearly every poltergeist case, the strange events center around one person. Usually, it is a young person between the ages of 10 and 20.

At the warehouse, there was a 19-year-old shipping clerk named Julio Vasquez. Items crashed to the ground when Julio walked through the warehouse. If Juilo did not come to work, nothing unusual happened in the building.

Two researchers spent several days in the warehouse. They noticed that the items always fell in a counterclockwise direction. More objects fell closer to Julio and fewer fell farther away. There seemed to be an invisible whirlpool of energy around him.

Sometimes the poltergeist follows the young person from place to place. This happened in Sauchie, Scotland in 1960 to 11-year-old Virginia Campbell. At first there were tapping, knocking, and sawing noises in her home. Some of the furniture moved on its own.

A few days later, things began to happen at her school. One afternoon her teacher saw Virginia trying to hold down the lid of her desk. The lid seemed to be opening on its own. An empty desk near Virginia slowly rose about an inch off the floor. Then it gently settled back down. The teacher checked the desk. She found nothing that could have made it move.

For a while, Virginia stayed with relatives in another town. The loud knocking noises were heard in that house, too.

Many psychical researchers believe that a poltergeist is actually a kind of **psychokinesis** (sy-ko-kin-ee´-sis).

Psychokinesis is the ability to move objects without touching them.

The young people in poltergeist cases usually are unhappy. They may be feeling tense, angry, or frustrated. They are unable to talk about their feelings.

Julio, for example, was unhappy with his job and did not like his boss. Virginia had recently moved to the home of her brother and his family. She was angry about the change. She missed her old home and her pet dog.

Some researchers believe that it is the young people themselves who cause the events. They probably do not realize what they are doing. They cause the events because they have such strong feelings.

In 1972, a group of Canadians did an experiment that seemed to prove people can create a poltergeist. Eight members of the Toronto Society for Psychical Research decided that they would try to produce their own ghost.

The members made up a personality and invented a life history for him. They decided what he looked like. One member even drew a picture of him. They called their ghost Philip.

For an entire year, the group met every week. They sat around a table and quietly thought about creating Philip. Nothing happened. Then they tried something different. They sang songs, told jokes and talked to the table. At the next meeting things began to happen.

The table started vibrating. It made knocking noises. It began answering questions from the group by rapping once for "yes" and twice for "no."

As the group continued its meetings, the table moved more. It tipped up on two legs and slid around the room. It floated with all four legs off the floor. One evening, it chased after a group member who was leaving. It ended up wedged in a doorway.

The Canadians were able to do the same things with other tables in other places. They showed off their "poltergeist" for a television program produced in Toronto. They also traveled to America to show their frisky table to scientists in Ohio.

The members of the group believed they had created a poltergeist with their own energy. Perhaps other people—without knowing it—can do the same thing.

# Talking to Ghosts

Some people believe a ghost is the soul of someone who died. The person may have had a sudden or violent death. He does not realize that he is no longer alive. He may wish to remain because he has unfinished business or does not want to leave his loved ones.

People who say they can talk with these spirits are called **mediums**. Mediums claim they can see and hear ghosts. They know what the spirits are feeling. Mediums say they can go into a trance and allow the spirits to speak through them.

A person living in a house that seems to be haunted sometimes will ask a medium for help. The medium "contacts" the ghost. A medium finds out why it has stayed in the house. Mediums believe that with a little nudging, the soul can be persuaded to move on to its new life. Then the house is no longer haunted.

One story about a ghost and a medium is told in the book *This House is Haunted*! The author of the book, Elizabeth P. Hoffman, says this experience actually happened to her family.

It began when the Hoffmans bought a large old house in Beechwood, Pennsylvania. A few days after moving in, 6-year-old Wynne was sleeping with his pillow over his head.

"Mommy, a lady comes in and looks at me after you turn out the light," Wynne told her. "She just looks at me. I can't sleep with her watching me, so I just put the pillow over my head. Then I can't see her."

Soon all of the sharp knives and scissors in the house began disappearing. When new knives were bought, those disappeared too.

Hoffman's mother also moved into the house. She complained that someone was walking up and down the hall outside her bedroom at night. When she looked out her door, no one was there.

Hoffman's daughter saw a strange woman in an old-fashioned dress standing in the upstairs hallway. Cats raised their backs to be petted when no one was there. A rocking chair in one room rocked back and forth for an hour at a time, even though no one was sitting in it.

Family members started calling out names. They asked the ghost to stop. The strange events continued.

"Then one day I was playing the piano when I heard a breathing sound in the music room," Hoffman writes. 'Go away, Clara,' I said. 'Please go away.' The breathing stopped!"

From then on, they called their ghost Clara. Hoffman did some checking. She discovered that the house once had been owned by a woman named Clarinda Johnson.

Finally, the Hoffmans asked the famous medium Eileen Garrett for help. Garrett walked into their home and said, "Your Clara is here. I see her and feel her. I will speak for her."

Garrett walked into the music room and sat down in the chair that always rocked by itself.

"She closed her eyes and began to speak. She lost her own Irish accent and began to speak with a New England accent," Hoffman writes.

Through Garrett, the Hoffmans found out that Clara was a widow when she moved into the house. She had a son and a niece. Another son had died when he was little.

Later, her only son was killed in an accident. The people in the town did not like Clara. She had no friends. She still lived with her niece, but was lonely and unhappy.

One day, Clara was going down the narrow cellar stairs. She fell and badly injured her head. She was afraid a doctor would need to operate on her head. She hid all the knives and scissors in her house. She refused to get help and an infection developed. This led to her death.

"But her spirit, being very confused and still needing love, didn't leave the house" Hoffman writes. It still looked for knives and scissors. Or it paced up and down the hall as she had done when she was alive and in pain."

Following Garrett's advice, the Hoffmans and a few friends sat in the music room two or three times a week. They prayed for Clara's rest. They talked out loud to Clara. They told her that they loved her and wished her well. They said it was time for her to leave the house and go on to her new life.

After several months, the footsteps, rocking and other ghostly events stopped. Clara was gone.

# Phantoms of Film

There are hundreds of photographs showing what are supposed to be ghosts. Many were taken during the late nineteenth century. Photography was still new. Most people at that time did not know how easily a photograph could be changed.

Now when we look at the photographs, it is easy to see that they are fakes. The "ghost" is really someone dressed in veils or sheets. The photographer added a blur when he printed the photo. Some photographers even created portraits of their customers with a "ghost" by printing two negatives together.

However, there are a number of ghost photographs that are not so easy to explain.

One was taken at Raynham Hall, a stately mansion in Norfolk, England. This house was said to be haunted. Visitors said they had seen the ghost of a woman wandering through a hall in the mansion. She wore a long, brown satin dress. Her face had an eerie glow but no eyes.

Captain Provand and Indre Shira came to Raynham Hall, to take pictures of the mansion for a magazine.

The two men were setting up their camera to take a picture of the main staircase in the house. Suddenly, Shira shouted that he could see the ghost of a woman coming down the stairs. Provand, who was busy adjusting the camera, quickly took a picture.

When the photograph was developed, it showed a pale, transparent shape in the stairs. It looks something like a woman wrapped in a veil. The details of the face or clothing are not clear.

Photography experts who checked the original photograph said that it did not appear to be a fake. The figure is so vague that it may have been caused by a defect in the camera or the film.

Another famous ghost photograph, called the Tulip Staircase, was taken by accident, too.

In 1966, two Canadians, Reverend Ralph Hardy and his wife, were visiting the Queen's House, in Greenwich, England. The house was built by King James I for his wife, Anne of Denmark.

Inside the house, Reverend Hardy took a picture of an interesting stairway called the Tulip Staircase. He and his wife saw no one on the stairs when the picture was taken.

On the photograph, however, there is the faint image of a person in a robe climbing the stairs. A hand with a ring can be seen holding the handrail. Some people say they also can see a second or even a third figure on the stairs.

Reverend Hardy and his wife were not interested in ghosts. They sent the picture to some psychical researchers. Photography experts said it did not look like someone had changed the film.

Television cameras have tried to capture ghosts, with some strange results. In 1964, an NBC film crew went to Great Britain to make a television special called "The Stately Ghosts of England." One of the haunted houses chosen for the program was the manor house at Longleat.

The Marquess of Bath, whose ancestors lived in the house, told them the story of Lady Louisa Carteret. Louisa married in 1735. She was not happy with her husband. One evening, a dance was held at Longleat. Louisa met a young man. She fell in love. When her husband found out, he was very angry. He and the young man fought a duel on the third floor of the house. The lover was killed. Louisa died a short time later. Some said she died of a broken heart.

For years, people said that strange things happened in the third-floor hall where the duel was fought. This is where the NBC crew set up its cameras.

In his book, *Haunted Houses*, Larry Kettelkamp tells what happened:

"From the very beginning, they had mysterious problems. Roll after roll of color film was developed and showed nothing at all but yellowish or greenish haze. New cameras were brought in, and new film stock was tried with no better results.

"Automatic equipment had been set up to shoot film footage during the night. It would be found inexplicably shut off the following morning. The tapes from tape recorders were as bad as the muddy films. Unusual accidents began to occur. By itself, a reflector floodlight rolled out of a bedroom, down a hall, hit a banister, then fell over it to crash down the open stairwell. It almost hit an NBC crew member. Other lights blew up, and the telephones went dead. It was reported that during an attempt to film a grandfather clock striking midnight, every other clock in the house struck the hour except the one that was being photographed. A crew member made some sharp remarks about the clock, and the next day, he was in an automobile accident.

"Finally the film director tried a new approach. As strange as he felt about it, he walked into the third-floor hall and said to the ghosts, 'I believe you are doing this. If you want me to ask your permission, I do humbly ask that you permit us to put this story on film.' After that, the trouble stopped. A special camera on the third floor filmed a most unusual sequence. This camera had been set to take shots automatically at intervals during the night. When the time-lapse shots were developed, there was a sequence in slow motion. It showed a light like an automobile headlight coming out one door, moving down the hall, and then disappearing behind another door. Nobody could figure out any logical explanation for the light."

# Fact or Fantasy?

Do ghosts really exist?

Researchers have been trying to answer that question for hundreds of years.

As far back as 1665, there was a group in England that studied reports about ghosts. The club included some of the most educated men of the day.

Today, the search for answers continues. In the United States alone, about 40 groups study ghosts and other supernatural subjects. Research is also being done at several colleges and universities.

Other groups try to prove that ghosts and other supernatural events are nothing but hoaxes. One of these groups is headed by a magician named James Randi. In a number of cases, Randi has shown that strange "supernatural" events were really tricks.

Millions of people still believe in ghosts. Not long ago a research group asked people all over the United States about ghosts. Forty-two percent of those people—almost half—said they believed they had been contacted by someone who was dead.

Could that many people be mistaken?

In some cases, people were probably imagining things. Our eyes and ears can play tricks on us. This is especially true when we are upset or tired, or when we are just falling asleep or waking up. Maybe this is why so many people see ghosts when they are in bed.

Psychologists (si-kol´-oh-jists) who study the mind tell us that people sometimes see what they want to see. This is especially true during very difficult, emotional times—for instance, when a person's husband or wife dies. This could explain why nearly two-thirds of the widows and widowers in the survey said they had been contacted by their dead spouse.

Other ghosts are not as easy to explain away.

Proving that ghosts exist, however, is very difficult. For one thing, ghosts rarely show up when people want them to. Often when they do show up, some people see them and others do not.

Some researchers have tried to capture a ghost on a photograph, movie, or tape recording. Even when they managed to record an image or a sound, other people weren't convinced. Film and tape recordings are easy to fake. Today, researchers use more complicated instruments, like infrared cameras and geiger counters. They have found some interesting things, but nothing that is definitely a ghost.

Most of the time, researchers have to depend on what people tell them about ghosts. Unfortunately, this is the worst way to prove ghosts are real. Some people say they see ghosts because they like to get attention. Others try to make money by making up a ghost story and claiming it is true. Even people who really believe they have seen a ghost may have been fooled or may be mistaken.

Someday, scientists may find a way to prove whether or not ghosts exist. Until then, we have no answers, only unexplained experiences and interesting guesses.

# Glossary

**Apparition:** A strange or unexplained vision.

**Hallucination:** Seeing or hearing something that is not real but created in the mind.

**Haunt :** To bother with constant visits, actions or activities.

**Mediums:** People who are able to contact and communicate with the spirits of the dead.

**Mental Telepathy:** The ability to communicate without using sight, sound or actions....a transfer of thoughts.

**Parapsychologists:** People that investigate supernatural phenomena.

**Poltergeist:** A ghost that is usually noisy or responsible for noises.

**Psychical:** Being able to understand the forces beyond the physical world.

**Psychokinses:** The ability to move objects without touching them.